TALES OF MAGIC

SHORT STORIES TO IMAGINE

DHRITI

This book is dedicated to my family members who constantly supported me to pursue writing books

Contents

I

Believe in the unbelievable

Tina , A 12-year-old girl, always believed that fairies exist and because of their very existence the world is so vivid and magical. On the contrary Tina's father did not believe in fairies nor their existence. One bright morning when Tina was playing in a playground of a broken park she fell and hurt herself. Suddenly something happened that shocked Tina . She found shimmering dust all the way to a dusty old House which was quite creepy. But, Tina was a brave girl so she took the risk of going inside. She was astonished to see a heap of sparkling dust lying down on the floor of the house. She started to somewhat imagine maybe it was the house of the fairies. Out of curiosity she explored here and there and finally found a small round black tunnel that led somewhere . She quickly jumped inside that tunnel and slipped through the dark. She now reached a destination , perhaps never seen by humans. It was a wonderful place. She was shocked to see butterflies talking with each other, fighting with each other for sweet nectars of a giant flower! Those butterflies were just so colourful, They had enormous wings with beautiful patterns. As Tina moved further she saw cats and dogs living together in harmony, peacefully having a tea session! The roads were made of candies and trees of chocolate. She then saw a gigantic pulchritudinous castle . Though the surroundings were bright, cheerful , vivid the castle was pitch dark , it was made of thorns just like the moors of Maleficent .As she was about to enter the castle a group of unidentified species came and took Tina away from the castle . They dropped Tina on a golden cloud .Tina who was frightened as a scared cat and spoke , "Who are you all and why did you bring me here ? " She heard a tiny , pristine voice speak out . Hello human , I am the head of fairies , My name is Myra . I have rescued you from the shadows of dark ferrows..

Tina, who was literally confused, asked Myra to explain the situation. Myra spoke now in her deepest tone . She said ,The place you are looking at is the dreamy land , we all live in harmony. This place is so beautiful, here there is no corruption, Arguments . This was all until the dark Ferrows rules decided to show up. They took over our land , killed a few fairies and are trying to change this place into a hell,where evil takes over good ." Tina , who got the matter crystal clear now spoke,Being a human and to extend my hand as a friend I , Tina a human being , is willing to help the fairies. " Myra laughed a bit in her formal way but she knew Tina was the best person to help her . So in the few weeks Myra made Tina act as a fairy , walk and fly as a fairy and even talk in the lightest tone possible just like a fairy ! Then Myra gave Tina her final training which was the act of dressing in such a manner that the ferrows will get deceived by her looks. When Myra could trust her entirely she made Tina talk to the rest of the fairy family . They were cute , beautiful and strong . Just as the final training they were pretty light from outside but then they proved how strong they were just by making their looks cute. Now all prepared, the fairy army flew towards that dark castle and towards the face of danger . Some of the fairies went left while others went right .Tina and Myra were leading the group . Somehow they gained access against their defense system but the real danger lies in fighting the head of Dark Ferrows. He was a formidable man who knew black magic and knew how to read someone's mind . So as the fairies had discussed everyone starting to sing it became difficult for the dark ferrow to understand their strategy , the only thing he could read was the lyrics of the song from everyone's mind . The dark ferrow gave up and left their land without any second thought .After accomplishing their mission everything went back to normal . Peace and harmony reigned . The fairies told Tina that they were obliged for her actions and were willing to repay whenever she needed help. Thanking the fairies for this magical opportunity ,Tina got her way out and never saw that house again . One day , Tina and her father as usual had a heated conversation about supernatural beings including the fairies. Tina who was at the verge of losing remembered that the fairies could be called to help , she summoned them and magically Myra appeared and made Tina's father realise he was wrong .She told , when there is good there is evil . Humans(some of them) tend to destroy earth but fairies work together to restore the perfectly serene nature of earth. When there is a demon then there are angels. Her father related to whatever she said and told her never to argue about them . Like this Tina who was only 12 years when she made her father believe in the unbelievable.

II

A sneak peek in my life (Author's life)

So first of all My name is Debangana Sengupta, a normal middle schooler who finds the world quite abnormal to fit in . The covid has changed me a lot starting from adopting new hobbies to finding old toys and even washing dishes . I have figured out that doing things in an individual manner is much better than in groups of friends because they always have been betraying me . From the beginning of 2019 Lockdown gave me a varied insight in Music. I discovered different genres of music . I found my soul in the voices of singers like Olivia Rodrigo , Charlie puth , Roseanne park. At this very time I understood we should always give importance and respect to a person till that person is near us . I sometimes feel distant from other people but that's okay . Unfortunately we all can't understand this feeling . The law of life and the Homo sapiens are quite distorted in their own way . As a teenager I considered life to be uncertain and full of mysteries. This is the main reason why I love reading and writing fiction stories because it helps me escape reality and find a new home that is so alluring. My parents are so considerate and always cheer me up whenever I feel low . Every time I achieve something, be it the smallest in size or not so grandeur, they always feel proud of me . Their endless sacrifices have built me a person whom I stand today .Maybe a person is born imperfect but there are the standing pillars of someone's life that makes them seemingly perfect . As always I wouldn't forget to mention my maternal grandparents. They have always been the best . My grandma and grandpa were always there when I needed help , they never scolded me and always gave me a second chance to improve . They always said it's not necessary to become a billionaire but to become a good person ,lawful citizen , friend, daughter and an obedient student . They have been inspiring me to do more creative work in my life . My grandparents were the happiest person I saw as I published my very own first book . So, firstly let me give you all a small sneak peek into my hobbies . I have been pursuing classical form of dance (Odissi) for over 10 years , then I had a small experience of classical music for about 5 years .And then suddenly came my inspiration of drawing , first it started with oil pastels and then as time passed by I progressed immensely and reached my goal of sketching and watercolor my next goal is to start with oil painting. I always welcomed new ideas but soon enough I lost interest in them. These are a few of my hobbies which I still have my interest in . Before I used to take swimming lessons and badminton lessons but I got bored and left. Then I tried out abacus but my studies became a lot heavier than it was so I left abacus training. Now I am looking forward to learning guitar because somewhat I consider guitar gets you a style in your perspective and also you get a bit more tuning in your songs . I won't forget to mention my best friend's name. Her name is Simi and we together are called bestie Gang .So this is my sketchy life where I have tried out a lot of things, seen failure and also success. I hope that after you go through my stories I may be able to increase your imaginative skills .Thanks a lot for listening to my life story and I expect my readers to engage into story writing and I will be eagerly waiting to read their stories .Let's resume back into storytelling!

(I hope you will like reading my stories)

III

A Detective story

Life is an ever-ending Enigma. Sometimes we learn something or we leave behind imprints of intellect that may come in help for the future generation. This world is full of mystic beings, the almighty send people here to teach us something or to learn new things and return back to God . Similarly, he sent a few gems on this earth who created a special place here and made a difference that no one else did. Let me tell you today a story of a masterpiece created by a mastermind that got stolen wantonly by a thief. The history behind the stolen masterpiece starts from the early 1450 s when a child with excellent intelligence and artistic skills was born. He was no ordinary child, yes he was indeed a gem sent by God to teach us lessons that we were overlooking. Yes, I am talking about Leonardo Da Vinci whose birthplace is in Anchiano, Italy. He was a man of varied interests. Not only was he a painter but also a sculptor, engineer and scientist. His creations created an enormous influence during the Renaissance, One such masterpiece was "The Mona Lisa" painting still found in the Louvre museum of France. We do admit it's something that has a unique essence.

One fine wintry morning when everything was going well , a welsh girl residing in the Streets of Rue de Rivoli Paris started her day with an exciting call. Arona, a 16 -year-old girl picked it up and was excited after their conversation. Arona was called by the headmistress of the Aristocracy school. She was picked as an escort for a group of students sent on a trip to the Louvre museum, a place of flourishing artworks that are preserved there from the time of Renaissance in Europe. She got up early, in the morning with a super smiley face and an energetic mind. She dressed herself in proper attire and set out for her assigned work. As she reached the museum, she greeted the group of children with a warm smile. As she walked inside the museum explaining the history behind each masterpiece, they heard something terrible. The Mona Lisa painting has been missing since this morning. It sounded quite absurd because there was not a single clue of the thievery . It was so well executed. The place was sealed but somehow the Police allowed Arona to take a peek in, as Arona belonged to a well reputed Welsh family. When Arona was observing she stumbled upon something and she saw that there was a laser sensing torch. This made it very clear that the person used it in the process of stealing the painting . Suddenly, another case happened that astonished all . The world's largest Ruby got stolen . Arona started to find connections between these two cases. The Mona Lisa painting which is worth millions was bound to be robbed innumerous times. This was the 10th robbery . Arona noticed that bits of papers were also lying in the corner of the room . When she looked at it closely she was totally confused as those papers were bits of documents about the Security room of The Louvre. Now, She saw the connections,that these papers might be used by the thief. The police, impressed with her pragmatic mind, allowed her to investigate further in the case. After escorting the children back to their school She went through the Criminal record diaries in the national library. She was shocked to see that the last time the painting went missing the police somehow found the criminal in Bedford but that criminal was a wrongly suspected person. The real criminal escaped and is thought to be living somewhere secretly in Bedford. Arona with full determination now set out to Bedford thinking she might actually find the real criminal behind the thievery . In her normal schedule for the first time something unusual was taking place. Arona excitedly reached Bedford thinking that she might find some clues. In Bedford she was surprised as she heard that the people living there were living a life of nightmares because a lot of thievery was taking place. After a lot of searching She reached the most secretive Part of Bedford; it was the great " Woburn " which was quite distant from the usual city life. Crime was born there. Alongside Woburn is a forest where Arona started her search . As Arona headed deep into the forest she found footprints along with bits of papers lying in a certain direction. It now made very clear that the criminal was certainly hiding somewhere in the deep of the forest from the hands of the law. After walking a mile or so Arona discovered a wooden house. Out of curiosity Arona thought of having a peek into the house. She found something that was unbelievable, she found the Mona Lisa painting, yes, certainly it was the very own creation of Leonardo daVinci. She was starstruck to find the world's largest ruby inside a wooden crater. Suddenly a creaking sound of the wooden stairs was made. Aruna quickly took action and hid beneath the bed in the bedroom. She encountered a man of her age coming inside the room with a gun probably, it was an unofficially purchased one. The man's reflexes were quite sharp so he easily found Arona hiding beneath the bed. The man took out the gun from his pocket and pointed it towards Arona, Arona who has been taking self-defence classes quickly took the gun from the man's hand and pointed it back towards him. Now Arona made sure that the man speaks each and every word that was indeed about the thievery he did. The man having no choice spoke ," I am just a commoner who is different from others, I am a kleptomaniac who has tendencies of stealing things. From my very childhood I had a fascination about the Mona Lisa painting, it's just mysterious yet charismatic, it holds mysteries that are still unsolved. So my wish was to get a closer view to the painting. My family, persistently told me if I wanted something I should definitely get it ,unexpected of the various dangers which lie, I stole the painting. It is not because I'm a criminal but I am an enthusiastic person who wants to learn the secrets of painting." Now Arona spoke, "but why did you steal the world's largest ruby ?" The man spoke," I always wanted to have precious jewels which would make me somewhat popular in my area .From the very beginning I have been neglected in society so I always wanted to prove to them I was worthy, I had the potential." Arona understood the situation and assured him that no one from now on would disrespect him.

Impressed with Arona's kindness without even thinking twice ,the man gave the ruby and the painting which was worth millions, in the hands of Arona. Thanking the man,She headed straight to the police station, explained the situation to them and handed over the lost items to them. The entire police station gave a salute towards Arona's bravery and pragmatic mind. She was even awarded by the

Louvre museum. The painting still thrives to be a powerful and pulchritudinous artwork with secrets that are undiscovered.

IV

The Game

Andre , Philly and George were planning to buy the latest game set but they knew it was impossible to get a game set within their budget .They have been friends since Nursery. Coincidentally they always got in the same class , section and moreover they lived in the same colony. Their bonds were unbreakable . Soon it was Andre's birthday. As all of them faced the harsh truth of not having enough money so they couldn't find a perfect gift within the suitable budget ($10). While walking down an old lane called the Victorious lane George found a very peculiar looking coin . There were silver marks along with gold on it . It said , " Each coin has the perfect value." He picked it up and continued walking . On his way home he found a small vending machine not containing juices or food stuff . It contained a game set . The game set looked colourful and cool too. So he thought to get the game set moreover it was within his budget . When he tried to enter the $10 coin through the provided area it didn't enter . He was shocked as well as confused. Soon he remembered he had got an unusual coin in his pocket , he took it out and placed it inside . This time it went inside ! The vending machine started to make noises like Hurray ! You got the bumper price or Congratulations for receiving the brand new game. Suddenly he found another coin on the ground. He picked it up . All of this made George feel ecstatic . He continued going home by singing a song , hoping like a grasshopper. Once he reached home he called Andre and Philly to come over . He told them the entire situation that took place and how he managed to get a game set for Andre within the budget of $10. Andre was in cloud nine he never touched or even got the thought of getting a game set on his birthday . Days passed by after this incident occurred . Three of them decided to go on an adventure which included discovering new places in their creepy neighbourhood which no one wants to go to .Philly got himself a dusty old plastic which he covered himself to look like one of the plastic superheroes ,Andre carried the game set he got on his birthday , George carried some food stuff so that they don't have to starve . They started the journey around 6 o'clock in the morning and reached a very dark and creepy area around 12 o'clock in the noon. Things got even creepier when they discovered a dead body lying in front of a huge bungalow which was grey and looked like Satan's home . Philly spoke with a sotto voice , ". I think we should return back home. This isn't safe and moreover there are no people around." George was laughing at whatever Philly said. He said, "You are acting like a mouse. Come on Philly, you have grown up so much next birthday you turn 14! You can't act like an immature boy." Three of them were actually internally screaming because of fear but none of them wanted to show it. To divert this creepy topic Andre started running towards the house when he reached the door, the door flung open. He felt apprehensive but he went inside. Seeing him the other two boys also went inside and the door closed with a sudden noise. Andre took out the game set George gifted him. Three of them sat in a circle and were curious to see what's inside. They discovered an old map with a remote control and a black screen. Everyone felt clueless about how to play the game. Suddenly out of nowhere a piece of paper came flying out of a broken window pane and struck Philly's face. He unfolded the paper and read, "Dear gameplayers you are officially selected to play the Dragon‘s mouth. You may be wondering how to play the game at first so listen to my instructions . The map you see is a mystery map, It may be a map that guides you to a treasure or a map that directs you to the world of Hades which is the underworld. Beware if you by mistake go to the underworld you shall never return and see the light of the world we are currently living in . Second, the black screen you see helps you predict the future, for example if you are stepping on a wrong path the black screen turns into red and stops you but if you step on the right part the black screen turns green. Third, the remote control you see should be used only during emergency time because this remote control is no ordinary control device; it actually controls a far distant bridge between the fantasy and the non-fiction world. One wrong mistake and you are drowned! I hope you got the instructions clear, hoping to see you all get out of this game without dying. Three of them thought this was a chance for them to prove to everyone that despite their age they are quite mature. Andre took charge of the black screen, Philly took charge of the remote control, George took charge of the map because he used to get an A+ in his geography tests. George guided them to a place which was an old building with a staircase going up and down. George tried to go downstairs but suddenly Andre stopped him saying something is wrong you shouldn't go downstairs because the black screen turned red. On the other hand Philly was shaking badly, He was so frightened that he almost fainted. So everyone went upstairs, they found an old box made up of a combination of metal and wood and the lock made up of silver and gold. It was a rare sight. Andre tried to break the box but it wasn't breaking at all. Then George remembered that he got the game said by inserting a very odd coin and he still had that coin in his pocket he took it out and placed it inside the lock and the box bursted out. To their surprise it actually contain gold silver and even platinum coins. This was a chance for them to live a bright future with the treasure they receive today. Three of them walks happily down lane to their apartments and from then onwards lived a happy life . No, wait there is a twist The game set was left behind in the chaos . Do you think someone else is going to receive it and embark on a new journey ?

V

On a chilly Christmas night I found a boy on the street

Christmas is my favourite season, it is indeed a merry time when people come together and spend the most wonderful time together. Some moments are created which are magical and extremely important because they change our view completely towards life. These moments create an enigmatic impact on us and fortunately change ourselves forever. Such an incident literally happened in my life .

Christmas night was extremely cold in the Netherlands. I remember spending my day with a cup of hot choco coffee and a journal book to write. I woke up at 7 AM and went on doing household chores and took a rest on my beanie bag. It was quite plushy and comfortable .During the evening time with my comfy blazers on I walked out of my house.

I was wandering in the streets and suddenly I spotted a boy roughly my same age crying badly . He looked very simple but his facial expression depicted something deep .Iapproached him and asked him why he was crying . He told me every Christmas night his sister and he would see the vivid auroras in the sky flowing but this year his sister passed away. I felt very bad for him and comforted him.

In his eyes I saw his pain clearly expressing his deep down desire to meet his sister but unfortunately he can't meet his sister. I told him his sister now lived as a bright shining star in the sky blessing his brother from above . Saying this I asked him if he would like to accompany me in watching the vivid Auroras from a place very far from this distant city life . He agreed . Happily, I got my car out and took him to that place . It was truly a spellbound Moment , stars above us seemed to be calling upon us , the sky seemed to be a spectacular thing to watch . While I was watching its serene beauty I noticed him standing beside a tree and shedding tears of pain. I got him back and told him that life is full of uncertainty. We should welcome whatever awaits us because life goes on . My words somehow brought some hope in his eyes . He held my hand , we sat together down and watched the amazing beauty of the Auroras. Somehow the beautiful night passed very fast . I was about to bid him goodbye but to my surprise he wasn't there. I searched here and there but saw no one . I was alone and for a moment I thought he was a thief maybe and I searched my purse but my money was intact in it. Suddenly out of nowhere he emerged from a nearby tree running towards me with a beautiful Flower(Rose) . I felt dumbfounded. I was suspecting such a person for thievery . He was so sweet . I asked him why so suddenly he bought me a flower. He replied , " To me You are an angel ,An angel who comes to people in distress . As I am homeless all I have to give you in return is a flower , a flower is the costliest gift of nature and those who appreciate its huge value are indeed an angel ." For a moment the wind stopped. All I could hear was the sound of the movement of my heart . The grass on which I stepped in suddenly felt so soft . He stared at me for a while and then gave me a warm hug . He then asked me if I was willing to be his best friend. Without a doubt I said ,"Yes ." We went home . He said it's now his time to return to his home but I insisted him to stay , tears rolled down my cheek. Those memorable moments became a flashback in front of me. He said not to feel bad because he will come to my house every month . Days passed and it turned into weeks then months . He never turned up , I was worried. Hurriedly, I went to the same place where I saw him but I didn't find him there. I asked my nearby people but none of them could answer my question. Then I approached a very old man . He seemed to be around 60. I asked him whether he had seen that boy around . As soon as I finished talking his face turned pale. He told me the boy I was searching for died weeks ago in a fatal car accident. The old man was his doctor who tried to cure but failed in doing so . He added further saying the boy left a letter to him and said that it should be only given to a specific girl. As he didn't have any family I kept the letter with me . It seems to me you are his friend. Please take this letter from me . With a heavy heart he left . I read the letter it said

Dear Best friend ,

I hope you are doing well . I am so sorry I couldn't visit you . I was hoping to see you soon but I was so distracted from my personal loss I could not contact you . I wanted to tell you how much impact you showed in my life . You converted my misery into strength. You truly are an angel direct from heaven . I don't have much time left so all I want to say is stay safe , happy and forever be like this . I like you and your beautiful personality. Even if I don't survive, you will thrive to survive in my heart forever. I wish every person in this world had a friend like you .

Bye my friend. Maybe we will meet in another life where you become my sister .

Yours Lovingly

friend

This letter broke me in pieces from the bottom of my heart . His words seem to be piercing through my heart a million times. I would never ever forget such a friend like him . This is how two friends met and then separated their ways but never separated from heart .

VI

When writings became a reality

Once upon a time there was a girl called Sabrina. She was a country girl living in Alabama . She was a part-time writer and she used to write wonderful stories. One day she was working on a new story titled " The high school Drama ." She herself was a school dropout and her family couldn't do much for her education so this topic was kind of interesting for her to work on . Though she never went to school her writing skills got her into the international platform where she got plenty of support from reputed publishers. Her story started as " Destiny is never to be forgotten, it always has an amazing impact on everyone." Her start lines were always beautiful. Then she continued to write till the evening. Sabrina thought of taking a break from her tiring schedule. She turned on the radio and listened to some of her favourite classic songs. As her break was on the verge of completion , She suddenly got a call on her mobile phone from an unknown person. First she thought to decline it but her mind changed and she took the phone. This is the very moment where Sabrina's life changed forever. Her life takes an unexpected turn that never runs out of danger, she never knew what was laid for her but eventually she accepted it. The unknown person talked in a husky tone, " I am the CEO of real writing, Sabrina you are a very talented writer so would you like to take the opportunity of working for our company. I can assure you that you will be paid a very hefty amount ." Sabrina didn't think much because she was not getting paid enough for her work and her bills were due so without further thinking she signed up for the job. Little did she know that she had stepped on the wrong path. He gave her all the details but didn't mention the company's address. When she asked for the address he said that the job was for work from home purpose so she didn't require the address. He further explained that she was very much responsible for her character's life . Any wrong step Sabrina takes in writing her character of the story suffers. First she didn't get much of what he said and started completing her same story. This time she wrote something about the protagonist. She named the protagonist as Daniel . He was a hard working student and a superb Basketball captain, it is said if someone played for his team they would surely win. Next, Sabrina added some details about the female character. She named her Rose. Rose was a shy girl but she was an excellent artist, singer and a poetess . Sabrina now thought of adding a shocking twist in the story. After completing the base of the story that is all about how the school life went and all the interest they had developed. Sabrina gave Daniel a memory loss part (in the story). It is the very part where her life changes. Suddenly she received a call about her friend, he had faced a terrible accident and was now taken to ICU. She was definitely shocked to hear what happened. The next thing she did was to rush to the hospital, where she saw him lying on the bed. His awful condition made her cry badly . She tried to confront him about how the accident happened. She was even more shocked when he said he didn't know her. Perhaps, she had come to the wrong room. Sabrina was shocked and hurriedly got the doctor for the check up, with a heavy heart the doctor said, " As he has gone through a dangerous accident,he now suffers with memory loss , if he is lucky his memory would return within five minutes or maybe by the next day or next week or maybe after years all we can do is hope his memory returns soon . After hearing this Sabrina went running towards her house. She was heartbroken after all the years spent , now he has forgotten her because of the accident. Something clicks on the back of her mind. She is immediately reminded of Daniel who is suffering from the same case and has forgotten his friend Rose. She now understood The real agenda of the CEO's company and the warning he had given her. She immediately removed Daniel's memory loss part and rewrote it as Daniel got into a minor accident and recovered from the damage . Immediately she received a call from the hospital stating his memory had returned. With this she stopped writing and thought about quitting but then she got another call . The person on the other side of the call said Sabrina if you're thinking of quitting it's going to make you regret. As you have already uploaded the story file to me I can make changes in the story and make sure you and your friend never get out of this melancholic story. I have the power of turning you into characters . So, if you want to not regret your decision then change it or else be ready to face the dark future. He hung up. For the sake of her and friend's life she had to sacrifice something, do a little bit wrong to get the right out of it. Like this she got trapped into the fingertips of the boss and was never able to come out of it . Her life could only be saved if the boss's identity was disclosed.

(Author's note- Do you think there is still a chance of escaping her terrible fate ? Can her Friend help her by changing the story ?)(Maybe her friend is the boss itself ?)

VII

The most unusual story of Cinderella

We have always read the same old story about the wretched behaviour Cinderella received from her stepmother and stepsisters but this time the story has a twist. Instead of portraying a very good character which has the qualities of a wise and kind lady she plays a more dynamic and a surprisingly more contrary role in this story.Now this Cinderella works for the secret Cop community where they maintain peace in a particular place without revealing their name or work. Cinderella portrays a very charming, kind person from outside to the world while from inside she is the most dangerous Lady one has ever met . She lived in a place that was far away from city life . Her life schedule starts from 6 in the morning and then ends at 9 in the evening . We might be thinking what happened to her family? Well ,she lived separately because of her job and never had seen her family from the very day when she got assigned with secretive projects . One day she was called out for a meeting at the nearby library. Cinderella loved reading books so she considered this to be the most amazing meeting ever held . When she reached there She spotted a tall , Handsome man standing with the chief of the secret cop community (SCC). The chief then said , " Everyone meet our new member Eden. He is the prince of this kingdom and as he is the prince he will be having a lot of details about criminology here so we decided to include him . He further added, " He will be taking over Cinderella's position on the very next lunar Eclipse that is supposed to happen ." Prince's father(King) had fallen ill so a ball was arranged surprisingly on the very next lunar Eclipse . Every Maiden of the kingdom was asked to visit the ball. Cinderella thought this to be her only opportunity of killing the Prince so that her seat in SCC can't be taken . The entire day she was busy planning about her murder . In order for smooth planning she sneaked into the castle to get more pristine details of the Prince and where the ball will be held while doing so accidentally she bumped into the Prince. He couldn't recognise Cinderella because she was wearing a face veil. Still the prince got spellbound by her beauty . She had the perfect cat- eye and perfectly straight blond hair . The prince introduced himself as the minor apprentice there just to maintain modesty of his nature but Cinderella very well knew who he was and just played along. The prince offered Cinderella a quick talk and a cup of tea . Cinderella accepted the offer. She found this to be a very good opportunity to get to know him more . He told Cinderella that he feels bad for taking over her place but if she wants she can be his assistant. This angered Cinderella a lot . Because she considered herself to be first and second to no one. The prince , himself, invited her to the ball and also promised her to give her the most spectacular gown the kingdom has ever seen . He requested her to wear that gown and come . Then , she went to her house . Afterwards she started to feel very lonely so she decided to finally talk to her parents . The first time she called no one picked it up, the second time a rusty voice at the end said, " Hello." Cinderella then spoke, "hmm is it mum or dad ?" The voice spoke saying, " this is you Cinderella? We waited for your call for years . How are you darling ? Did you forget us ? It's me, your mother . Your father died long back." She was grief stricken to hear her father's news . Cinderella then spoke , " I am sorry mom don't worry I will come back to you . Today itself I quit my job. I really missed your lullabies and your own handmade songs you sang for me .I promise you I am never going to leave you ." Hearing this her mother was relieved and asked Cinderella to return home back on the very next lunar Eclipse . This was shocking because all the important dates were literally falling on The lunar eclipse.She cancelled her plan of killing the prince but her inner instincts pushed her to meet the prince in the ball . The very next day was the lunar eclipse and she received the gown from the gown maker . Her eyes were stuck on it, it was so beautiful like it had been directly delivered from Heaven. She wore the dress and went to the ball . Everyone, even the guards just looked at her and kept staring at her like she was an angel who came from some unknown land . For the first time in Cinderella's life she was the spotlight , attention's sweet centre . The prince was again spell bound by her beauty . He told her she looked ravishing . Cinderella tried to act confused because the prince first told her he was an apprentice . Then the prince remarked saying it was just a joke and also. He is the prince himself . She acted very cool. They danced and danced but she remembered she had to get to her mother's place . She hurriedly went out and left behind her glass shoes . Prince picked it up and asked the guards to search the place . He even searched the whole town but couldn't find her .All this time Cinderella was living peacefully with her mother . The prince took an oath he wouldn't marry anyone but her . Lot of years passed by and the prince still didn't marry. He was still keeping hope that he might find her one day .

{ Re- publishing my first book - In search of the silver medallion }

VIII

Emelia smells a mystery

Emelia turned 16 years old the previous week. She got a bunch of presents: a gold ring, a pink dress with an unicorn badge which was just enthralling, a goldfish (whom she named goldie), an unicorn customized pencil box, and all other unicorn stuff you can think of! She also got a mysterious box that had Greek inscriptions. Emelia had found that suspicious thing in an empty canal near her house. As time passed by she felt more curious and after all her futile tries to keep herself calm she couldn't hesitate but to open the box. The box was pitch dark from inside nothing to be seen and contained an antique rusted clock and a golden medallion. Emelia told herself, "I need to do some investigations on these things". Emelia's mother Georgina was a scientist who worked on crazy projects and activities which were just beyond imagination and out of the box. This year she was leading a department that was in charge of working on a project, life without oxygen.

Emelia's father John was a singer although his family never accepted his profession still he had aspirations to become one.

Emelia gathered an observing tool like the magnifying glass a white cloth and a notebook for penning her observations down. While she did the observations of the box and its contents she felt a strong feeling. When she turned back to see what was there she saw a strange creature crawling on her back. She was frightened and did several frolicking jumps. Emelia said "oh my goodness!" What is this thing? The moment she took a step back she landed directly on the antique clock and whoooooooosh of she goes, the creature cast a spell .

IX

Time machine

In a flash of moment, a vortex of wind appeared out of nowhere she saw herself sitting on a huge dome-shaped vehicle entering a whole new world. The moment was so fast she didn't get the time to even realize what was happening. For Emelia, it was a sudden terror she had seen in movies. Suddenly there was a creaking sound. It sounded like something had collided against the land. When she opened her eyes she found herself stiff but to her surprise, she was wearing a beautiful dress nobody had ever seen. It was made up of a combination of silk and satin. She looked ethereal , from head to toe she looked like a beautiful maiden who had a great taste of fashion. Emelia found something on her clenched fist, it was the golden medallion she had last seen in her house. The mysterious creature took the form of a glorious figure. When the figure came in light Emelia stood astonished she was the goddess of great beauty, Aphrodite!

Emelia approached Aphrodite and said," O Great goddess of beauty please tell me where am I and what is happening?"Aphrodite said," No need to be afraid, my dear child you are the one chosen by the Greek gods. You need to help us solve the mystery. Athena, queen of great art and creativity chose you for your "patience, courage, ability". The goddess also added that she would be arranging the finest palace in the entire kingdom. Emelia gasped and said," Really! Firstly I am seeing gods then secondly I am the one chosen. Wait! Maybe I am just dreaming." She pinched herself to confirm but the pinch was of great pain. From the agony, she understood it was the reality and was very true! She continued in a sotto voice," what mystery?" Aphrodite said," You need to find the silver medallion, the one in your hand is the golden one. It makes sure that there is always justice, peace and mindfulness, happiness, and a good understanding. But without silver gold was incomplete. Silver makes sure that there is a good bonding between people, love, trust, and lasting faith". Emelia nodded her head giving a signal that she was looking forward to starting the mission. Before departing Aphrodite the greek goddess added," Guest from faraway

You must obey
Beware of the dangers ahead of you
As the medallion helps you to pass-through
Remember one thing morality and purity"

Saying this she dissolved into thin air. Emelia took the instructions of the goddess as a warning and continued.

X

A friend from the unknown

After experiencing the wealth of a greek palace and having the finest cuisines she had ever had. Emelia decided to have a quick tour of the back of the palace. While she was touring,she was also getting fascinated every moment, she spotted a forest which was quite unusual the forest was entirely made of pink trees and fruits made of gold and silver. Emelia saw something strange the silver fruits were starting to rot while the gold remained intact. She now realized the scenario it was all happening because the silver medallion was missing and if it was not found in time maybe the whole greek period might disappear. Without giving a thought of procrastination Emelia hurriedly went inside the forest for some clues which could be essential for her complicated mission. On her search she found a boy sitting near the roots of the tree with a melancholic expression. She asked him," who are you? Why are you sad?" The boy replied in a sotto voice," I am Euphurice an unlucky boy and an abandoned child." Emelia also got sad thinking about his condition she thought to give him a boost in his morale. Emelia said," Euphurice don't let the people get you ,come with me on my quest as no one knows maybe your unluckiness will turn lucky for me. Please be my Friend and a guide as I am absolutely new to this place." Euphurice was really encouraged by her words and agreed on her mission and to be friends.

XI

The enchanted woods

As soon as Emelia entered the woods Euphurice said that this place is full of riddles and mysteries and one will be killed if not solved on time . After hearing this Emelia felt nervous but carried on. Suddenly her surroundings changed, the ground started shaking and she saw that a giant tree was holding her and euphurice with their branches. The tree placed them on a rock, there were several of them which led to a magical portal . Everywhere it was water! Euphurice started panicking and Emelia tried to comfort him. Now the tree spoke " My name is Nayomi and I am the guardian who protects enchanted woods. No one has ever dared to enter this place but you have shown the courage which I appreciate. To get out of this place safely you need to answer my riddles , chances given to you will be 3 but if you fail you will die along with your friend a acidic water death because the water beneath you has high amounts of acids." Emelia felt apprehensive but instead of fearing she told her to ask her the riddles. Then the creature said," What can run but can't walk?" Emelia thought and thought and at the same point of time it started to rain. Suddenly her attention was drawn towards something. The heavy rain started flowing over the rocks and thus helping her to understand the answer of the riddle . She discovered that it would be water because water cannot walk but can flow. She told the answer to Nayomi who gladly allowed her to step on the second rock. The first rock got fully submerged in water . Nayomi now asked her " What has a face but can't smile?" After answering the 1 question correctly she gained confidence and didn't even think twice before giving her the answer . Emelia thought the answer would be human .Nayomi said the answer is wrong so as a punishment you have to stand on one leg until and unless you give me the correct answer. Meanwhile Euphurice also thought but didn't get any answer . Then, Emelia was reminded of something that she totally forgot it was about time . Immediately the time thing hit inside her head and she now related it to a clock . Now as she understood the answer she told it . Nayomi , smiling more than usual, told her to step ahead and also said this was her last question"What has 2 banks but no money? ". At last Euphurice said "Emelia I know the answer can I tell ". Emelia said that he can tell the answer. So Euphurice said it's a riverbank . Now , Nayomi smiled and said "You are free to go you really are intelligent and pure from inside ." Nayomi wished them luck and told them goodbye

XII

A Magic portal that leads to an ancient temple

The magical portal now lead Emelia and Euphurice to an ancient temple . When the sun's ray first fell on the temple it started to shimmer and glitter , the temple was made of pure gold and there were a lot of inscriptions and pictures that were displayed on the walls. As Euphurice knew how to read in Greek a bit he said that this inscription states that this temple is not an ordinary temple and it's a hundred years old temple. He also added that the inscriptions further say "beware of the dangers that lie ahead and use the gold medallion to pass through " Emelia now understood why at the beginning before leaving Great goddess of beauty Aphrodite told her that the medallion will help her to pass through. When she enters a part of the temple suddenly fire starts to blaze. Euphurice then, said Emelia not to step further as she did the fire stopped. Now it was simply clear that the temple was full of obstacles one has to pass through. Euphurice then said he had an idea that if they threw small things on tiles then they would be able to understand which tile is safe to jump on. Euphurice had some fruits which he threw on several tiles. At last one fruit that fell on a tile wasn't burnt so Emelia jumped on it. Like this they passed the first obstacle. Now they entered a new part where there was no floor ! Beneath them was water and bloodthirsty crocodiles.the only thing they had was a rope that was hanging from above . So Emelia took a risk and told Euphurice that they might not survive this obstacle but she will remember what he did for her. Saying this she took hold of the rope and ran backwards , she then came front and leaped forward in order to go to the other part . She did all of this by closing her eyes and only remembering her family. When she opened her eyes she was happy to find herself touching the floor of the other part of the temple. Euphurice was also smiling and thanking the lord. Then She climbed to the top and passed the rope back to Euphurice who did the same as Emelia did. After all they survived and the crocodiles were left behind hungry. Then she saw light coming from a distance. She ran towards it and found an exit ,again there was a magical portal that teleported her now to another place .

XIII

Journey to the wicked wizards lair

As the portal opened to another unknown place Emelia and Euphurice jumped out of it. After all the adventures they had gone through they needed rest. Both of their eyes dropped and then they fell asleep . Something was wrong! Few moments went by and Emelia woke up to find herself locked in a metal cage , she noticed the same happened with Euphurice who was madly struggling to get out of it. Emelia saw her golden medallion glowing brighter than ever. She took it near the cage and the cage melted. She was astonished and also freed Euphurice. They then started exploring the place immediately. Before they knew what was going to happen next they got surrounded by some people who had black marks on their faces and were wearing black hats , she now understood they were wizards not any wizards but dark magic Wizards. The wizards asked them to hand over the golden medallion to them, further they added "We will be powerful enough to defeat the great goddess of beauty Aphrodite , with the help of silver and gold medallion we will rule this world, Alas this world is ours" they remarked laughing cruely.

Now it was clear that the silver medallion was with them . Emelia refused to give them the medallion. Chaos rose, everywhere it turned black , plants started to die , nature was in great pain. Euphurice shouted to them telling," Hey! Wizards stop it now. I order you all my life I have been a coward but not now I and Emelia won't give up!" Emelia was feeling so proud for her friend. To her terror , the Wizards turned Euphurice frozen because they were angry . Now the Wizards turned towards her and walked in her direction. Emelia then took out her golden Medallion and said, I haven't given up, I know I can fight with you , the entire Olympus counts on me. I will take revenge from you all for my friend's death. Wizards! You don't know what trouble you have got yourselves in. Let's face it ." Saying this she holded her medallion high in the sky by aligning it with the sun rays it's power now became more and then she pointed it towards the Notorious Wizards who were immediately turned into ashes by the burning rays of the sun and the power of the medallion . she falls down crying for Euphurice.

XIV

A loss that cannot be replaced (death of Euphurice)

She bursted out crying . She admits that without him she couldn't have done all of this . All the adventures they embarked together made her fall more in love with him. She truly loved him and now wanted him. Suddenly a miracle happened, her tears turned into flower petals that covered all around Euphurice's body which melted the ice. After Euphurice gained consciousness he asked her "did we win?" Emelia now became emotional.It started Raining. She Confessed to him about everything she felt in reply Euphurice said he felt the same way. They hugged each other and cried amidst the rain. They promised each other that they will be like this forever no matter what happens. They stay together , fight together . Emelia asked Euphurice to accompany her back to her era when she returns home. Euphurice refuses saying maybe I can't go with you but nothing is impossible who knows we might meet again. Just believe in love, that's it. Now they took the silver medallion from the ashes of the wizards and returned back to the palace to meet Aphrodite and return the medallion to its rightful owner.They again traveled back through the portal and landed straight on the backyard of the Greek palace. Once they reached there they found Aphrodite accompanied with the Great Greek Gods -Athena, Zeus , Hera, Demeter, Apollo, Artemis, Ares,Poseidon, Hermes, and even Hades were there welcoming them .

XV

Returning the medallion to its rightful owner.

As they welcomed them back Emelia felt that she was on cloud nine . Now she took out the medallion and returned it to its rightful owner. Aphrodite along with the other Great Gods thanked her and Euphurice for fighting all odds in the adventures together Valiantly.Aphrodite handed over the silver medallion to Hades the king of the underworld and gave the golden medallion to Zues. It was distributed in this manner to maintain the equilibrium of earth and to spread peace and prosperity. Athena then came forward and said they were arranging a small celebratory dinner in order to celebrate the return of the medallion. So after Emelia and Euphurice refresh and rejuvenate ,Then they can meet them in the grand hall of the palace where this celebration will occur. After they took rest in a room Euphurice went out to see where this hall was while Emelia looked in the closet she was starstruck she found exotic dresses which had unique colour combinations and were made of soft material and they were just gorgeous. She quickly chose a new dress and went out ,everyone was enthralled by Emelia's looks . Euphurice was looking at Emelia as if he was spellbound by her . They danced and sang ate some awesome foods that Emelia hadn't even eaten before. Aphrodite noticed that how close Emelia and Euphurice was . So she thought of giving Emelia a little gift. It was going to be 12 PM at night and now the magic portal again showed up she now realised it was time she returned back to home as she successfully completed the mission. Aphrodite came forward and said," Dear Emelia, it has been a good time meeting you and I knew you had the potential from the very beginning. May you become successful in your life , I know you want to become an author then become one don't listen to what others say . Keep dreaming big and achieve your goals, just one more thing I know that Euphurice is somewhat became a very important part in your life as you love him so much so here, I am blessing you that maybe you can't take him with you but after you turn 26 you will meet him in your Era and then soon at the age of 30 marry him. May you have a great life ahead." Emelia then gave a smile and thanked all for choosing her for this mission. For the last time she shook hands with Euphurice and jumped into the magical portal. She was now travelling through an entire vortex of wind . A thud sound was made which bought Emelia back to sense. She now understood she was home. Her mom and dad had aged a lot more than she had seen before. She was surprised when they shouted "Happy Birthday Emelia you turned sweet 26 " Emelia stood still and realised this is the age Euphurice is supposed to meet her. Without overreacting, she hugged her mother and father saying that she missed them a lot. They were also happy but confused because they were around her all the time then how can she miss them . (If they only knew what actually happened to Emelia)

XVI

Home sweet home

As she was back home ,she ran upstairs and downstairs, explored here and there and opened all the gifts she received. For the first time Emelia accepted no place can be as good as a home. She remembered she had to note all of these incidents in a book. As she noted all the incidents in the book she thought to publish this. First she experienced the feeling of dejection but soon enough a publishing house finally accepted her talent and published it. Her writing bound everyone around the globe. She got so many compliments from people and developed a whole group of fans. She started receiving a lot of awards for her brilliant imaginative fiction writing skill . Her self- doubt turned into self- confidence. One day she was walking down the Lane thinking about Euphurice suddenly she hit someone, they both fell on the ground. Emelia stood up and said sorry for the inconvenience caused . To her surprise she had actually hit Euphurice. Euphurice immediately recognised her; they both cried after seeing each other for a long time. Emelia asked Euphurice what he was doing. He said that he was now a software engineer. They talked and talked for hours.

Emelia realised it was getting late so she took his number and quickly went back home. At home she started talking to Euphurice over mobile phones. As time went by Emelia finished writing a lot of novels which earned her the title"Queen of Novels". Her life was so perfect. Her parents also observed that Emelia spent most of the time on her phone. Soon she was 30. It was time she told her parents about Euphurice. Her parents acted really cool and said that they would first meet the boy's parents. Soon they all had a meeting and were quite satisfied about the decision. They agreed . The wedding bells rang in the church and everyone was so excited. The bride was accompanied by her father . Once the ceremony ended now they were officially married. Suddenly a lot of flower petals out of nowhere fell on the newly wedded couple. Everyone was surprised but they knew it was the great Greek gods blessing them for their reunion and big day.

XVII

Memories

They together formed a lovely family . Sometimes she was sad that she couldn't meet her parents often .During the cleaning of the house she found her childhood pictures which she showed to Euphurice. As she saw the pictures she cried and cried because she couldn't experience her childhood that much as there was a huge gap which she spent in the Greek world .There was something that she had to admit she had spent a magical life where anything was possible,Fighting wizards,giving answers to riddles and many more? Euphurice and Emelia held hands together and thought about that time in the Greek world they spent . Out of nowhere a piece of paper came into their room. Euphurice took it and read aloud ,"Dear Emelia and Euphurice I hope you all are doing fine. The Greek world is in Danger ,we need your help again . The dark Magic Wizards have somehow survived and are now planning to steal the crown of the magic fairies. So, Are you ready to take on this mission?" Emelia and Euphurice looked at each other and smiled more than usual. They were now ready to embark on a new journey to unravel mysteries.

I hope you liked reading my book.

9 798887 045948

Printed by Libri Plureos GmbH in Hamburg,
Germany